STAR WARS
BB-8 ON THE RUN

WRITTEN BY **DREW DAYWALT** THE AUTHOR OF *THE DAY THE CRAYONS QUIT*

ILLUSTRATED BY **MATT MYERS**

Disney • LUCASFILM PRESS

LOS ANGELES • NEW YORK

To Cathy, Chris, Kenny, and Debbie, who took me
to the movies —D. D.

For Vern, for making that cool spaceship for me
out of random model airplane parts —M. M.

The illustrations in this book were rendered in acrylic and oil paint with special effects
added in Adobe Photoshop.

Designed by Matt Myers and Scott Piehl

For information address Disney • Lucasfilm Press,

1101 Flower Street, Glendale, California 91201.

Printed in the United States of America

First Edition, September 2017 10 9 8 7 6 5 4 3 2 1

Library of Congress Control Number on file

FAC-038091-17198

ISBN 978-1-4847-0508-7

Visit the official *Star Wars* website at:

www.starwars.com

BB-8 wasn't used to being on his own.

And it was scary. **Very scary.**

His friend Poe had told him to run.

"Get as far away from here as you can,"
the pilot had said.

"I'll come back for you."

But BB-8 had seen the explosion back in Tuanul
village. And he feared Poe was gone....

Now it was all up to him to get the top-secret map
to the Resistance so they could find Luke Skywalker.

All up to him ...

That was scary, too.

As he took shelter for the night, BB-8 remembered something else Poe had once said to him.

"It's easy, buddy. You do good things, and good things will come back to you."

But how could such a small droid do such a big job?

The next morning, as BB-8 resumed his journey, he was glad to come across someone else. It was Teedo. But he was in trouble—his luggabeast was sinking into the sand.

"Please, help!" said Teedo in a language that sounded like screeches and warbles.

BB-8 was in a hurry to complete his mission, but he felt sorry for Teedo—and for the luggabeast, too.

Maybe BB-8 could do something for them....

OH, NO! IT'S A TRAP!

"I'm gonna take you apart and sell you, piece by piece," said Teedo. "You're even more valuable than the other one."

What other one?

A panel closed above BB-8, shutting out the sunlight.

He realized the only thing scarier than being alone in the dark . . .

...was *not* being alone in the dark.

Then the huge shape spoke....

"Please don't hurt me," it cried, trembling. It wasn't a monster at all—just a big, gentle loading droid.

BB-8 chirped happily at the massive thing.

"You promise?" it asked, worried.

BB-8 nodded wholeheartedly and beeped and warbled some more.

"Your name is BB-8?" said the loading droid.
"Mine is F3-ZK. But you can call me Fez."

The giant was no longer scared.

And BB-8 was no longer alone.

Fez told BB-8 he was part of a droid ship that was scouting Jakku. His ship was scheduled to leave that afternoon, but Fez was going to miss it because he was stuck in this cell.

Scheduled to leave that afternoon...

BB-8 was torn.

Should he stay on Jakku, in case Poe came back? Or should he try to get off the planet in Fez's ship?

The map had to be delivered, and soon.

But first they had to get out of this trap.

As BB-8 looked at a loose panel on the floor, he realized he had the perfect plan....

"Excuse me? Mr. Funny Little Lizard Man? We need your help," said Fez.

Teedo ran to see what was wrong. BB-8 was missing, and there was an opening in the floor.

"We were trying to escape and he fell in that hole," said Fez.

Teedo climbed into the cell and
looked down into the black space.

"I don't see him."

"Look closer."

Teedo bent over the hole.

"Closer," said Fez.

Teedo leaned waaaaay over the opening and peered in.

BEEEEEEEEEP!

With Teedo trapped, the two droids were able to escape!

"Let's get out of here so I can go home," said Fez. "You can come with me if you want."

HIGH FIVE

A VIOLENT YET FRIENDLY SLAPPING OF HANDS OVER THE HEAD TO INDICATE ACHIEVEMENT OR AGREEMENT. ALSO KNOWN AS HIGH THREE AND HIGH ONE AMONG VARIOUS SPECIES.

BB-8 let out a series of chirps.

"A mission?" asked Fez. "That sounds important. We'd better get you to the ship. It's picking us up at the Ruins."

BB-8 and Fez raced across the desert as fast as they could.

"The good news is, the funny little man is okay," said Fez as he noticed Teedo
in the distance. "The bad news is, he's following us."

Suddenly, a flock of angry steelpeckers flew up between BB-8 and Fez! BB-8 fled one way, and Fez went the other. The birds didn't know which droid to follow.

"Hey! Over here!" cried Fez, trying to get the steelpeckers' attention.

"Run, BB-8! You have to complete your mission!" Fez yelled. "I'll save you!"

BB-8 didn't want to leave his friend, but he had to deliver the map—and Fez was already leading the steelpeckers away.

Alone once again, BB-8 continued on his journey. He hoped Fez would be all right.

When BB-8 entered Kelvin Ravine, he met a scavenger family.

"Please, do you know where we could find something to eat?" asked the mother. "My children are hungry."

Was this another trap?

The children crowded around BB-8. When he saw their thin faces, he knew it wasn't a trick.

He remembered the food packets in the wrecked starship where he'd spent the night....
But it was in the *opposite* direction from where he was going.

If he hurried, he could get the family to the food and still make it to the droid ship before it took off.

If he hurried.

RATION

VEG-MEAT
POLYSTARCH
ACTIVATE WITH WATER
SEASON TO TASTE

RECIPE FILES

BB-8 hurried.

Next, BB-8 found a happabore with an injured leg.
BB-8 recalled the medical frigate he'd passed
that morning.

It would have first-aid supplies, but going back for
them would probably mean missing the droid ship.

BB-8 thought for some time, trying to decide
what to do.... The happabore moaned, and
BB-8 made up his mind.

Teedo was never going to catch him on that slow-moving luggabeast. BB-8 almost felt sorry for the weird little guy.

Almost. But not really.

BB-8 finally made it back to the happabore with a medical kit.

The beast was so happy it licked him and kissed him . . .

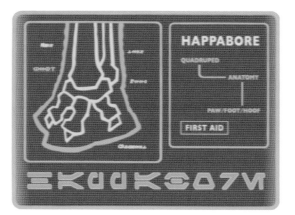

...which wasn't necessarily a good thing.

BB-8 worried that he was going to miss the droid ship because he had stopped to help so many people.

Just then, as he reached the Ruins, he saw something off in the distance....

THE DROID SHIP! At last!

Only, it was preparing to launch!

BB-8 raced for the ramp as it started to close.
Then he saw another wonderful sight. Fez!

Fez was okay! He had escaped the steelpeckers
and he, too, was running for the droid ship!

He waved happily to BB-8, who chirped with joy.
They were going to make it off Jakku together
after all!

But then something terrible happened....

Teedo appeared, blocking their way!

Fez started to panic, but BB-8 quickly formed a plan.
He remembered what Teedo had said—that BB-8
was more valuable than Fez.

He also remembered how Fez had saved him
from the steelpeckers.

BB-8 started to speed away from the ship, and Teedo followed BB-8 instead of Fez.

"Where are you going?" yelled Fez.
BB-8 beeped an order.

"Okay, okay, I'll get on the ship," said Fez.

"Thank you, BB-8! I'll never forget you for helping me."

The massive loading droid made it up the ramp just in time.

BB-8 felt he had done the right thing in helping Fez ... and the hungry family ... and the injured happabore.

But if he had done such *good* things, then why was this *bad* thing happening to him?

He was so confused.

Maybe Poe was wrong.

Maybe you don't get what you give....

Or then again, maybe you do.